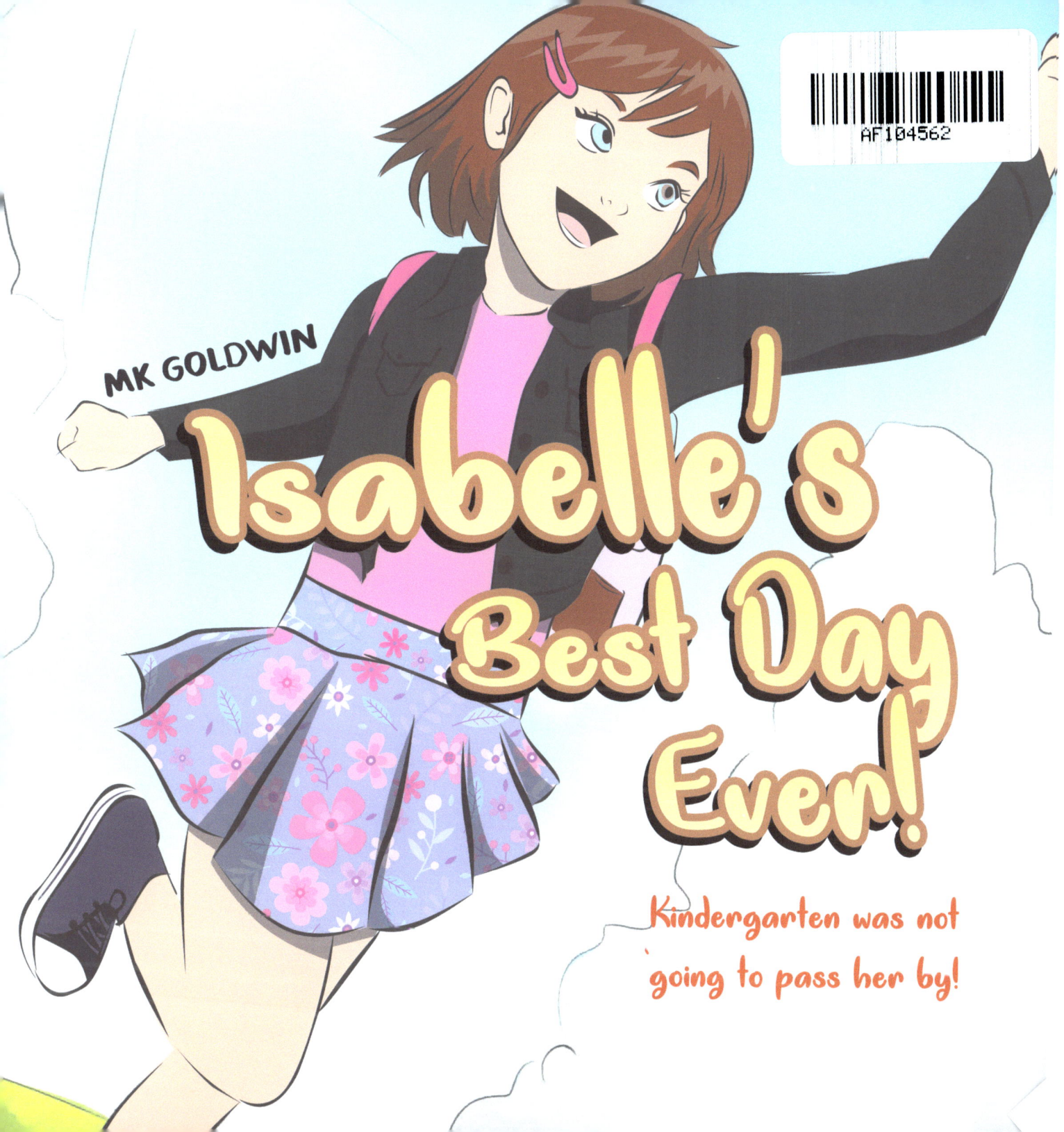

Isabelle's Best Day Ever!

Kindergarten was not going to pass her by!

MK Goldwin

Isabelle's Best Day Ever!
Kindergarten was not going to pass her by!

Copyright © 2023 by MK Goldwin

Paperback ISBN: 978-1-63812-689-8
Ebook ISBN: 978-1-63812-690-4

All rights reserved. No part in this book may be produced and transmitted in any form or by any means, electronic, or mechanical, including photocopying, recording, or by any information storage and retrieval system, without permission in writing from the copyright owner.

The views expressed in this work are solely those of the author and do not necessarily reflect the views of the publisher. It hereby disclaims any responsibility for them.

Published by Pen Culture Solutions   04/24/2023

Pen Culture Solutions
1-888-727-7204 (USA)
1-800-950-458 (Australia)
support@penculturesolutions.com

Sometimes little ones have struggles. This is the story of one little girl's struggle to go number two in a big person's toilet. Isabelle's struggle began well, the truth is, her family doesn't really know when it began.

After years of seeing kind, helpful doctors, wiping away buckets of tears, listening to countless words of encouragement, and finally accepting a struggle that could take a much longer time to resolve, with great relief, Isabelle finally had her best day ever!

At age two, Isabelle was already quite a uniquely adorable child. Her left copper-colored eye was lined with tiny specks of brown, and her right was a pool of crystal clear, blue water, kissed by the sun, set deep in a perfect heart-shaped face.

Her delicate physical features were certainly no match for her oversized imagination and quizzical fascination for all things technical.

When Isabelle's mommy and daddy were busy with everyday chores, Isabelle reached for any available technical gadget within range.

Her parents had programmed YouTube into their cell phones and tablets so Isabelle could access programs created to help children develop skills, such as recognizing letters and numbers and even singing along with the words to nursery rhymes.

This could be where Isabelle's struggle began. Perhaps when Isabelle was entertaining herself with YouTube videos or punching keys on the tablet, left unattended, her nimble little fingers stumbled upon stories where ugly monsters were swishing and swirling around the big white bowl before loudly being sucked down the drain! Perhaps the toilet monsters could even come back up through the drain and grab her little body!

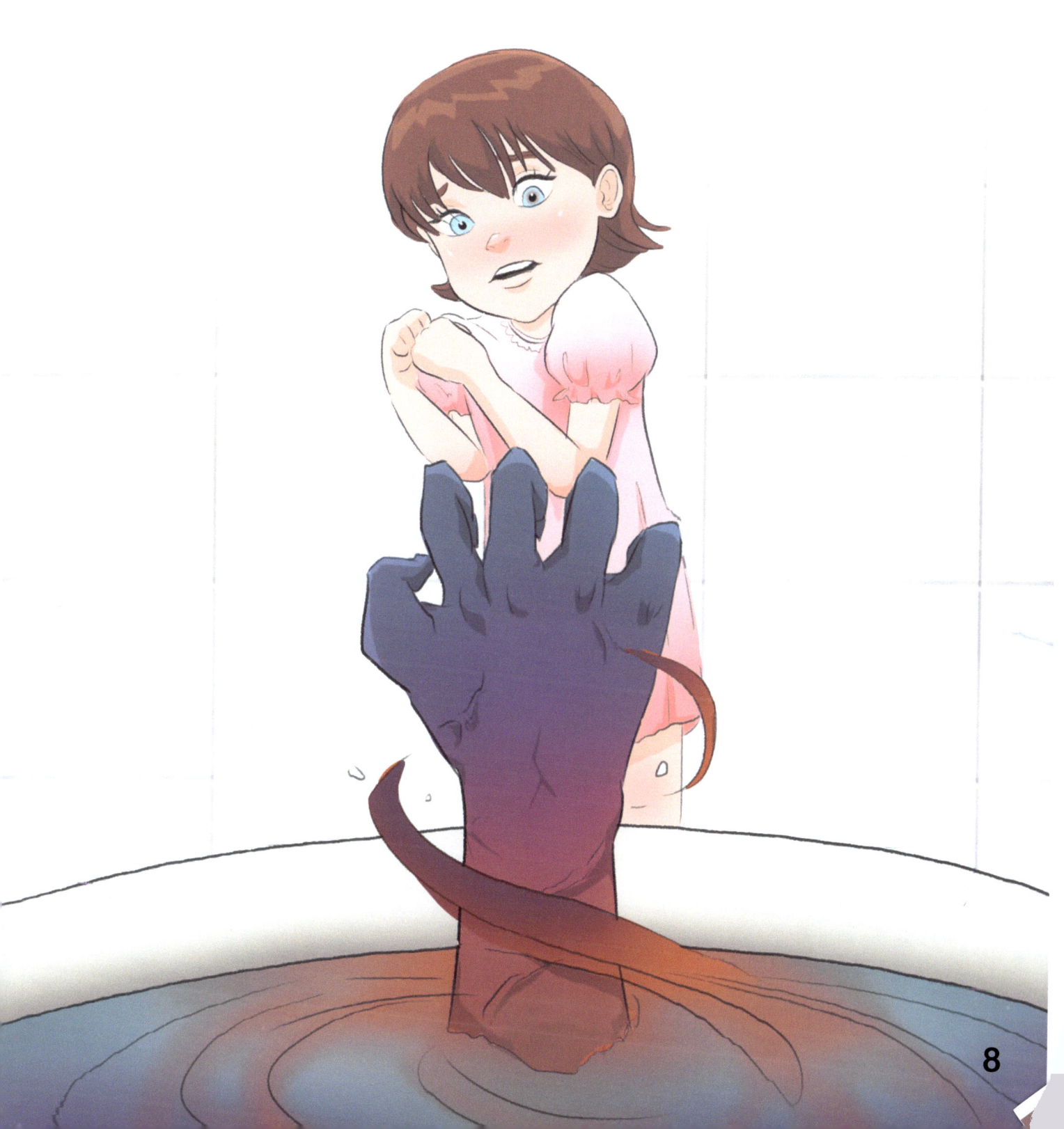

Despite the terror of being afraid to go number two, Isabelle flourished as a happy, well-adjusted child. Sunshine poked its bright yellow head into her bedroom window in the early mornings, and the moon's orangish glow tucked her into bed at night. Her days were jampacked with childhood lessons that help little ones become proud, successful adults.

By age three, Isabelle was proudly out of diapers.

Wait—not quite! Isabelle was so terrified of going number two in the big toilet that she had to squeeze into a diaper and hide deep in the back of a closet, where the quiet solitude allowed her to go number two in her diaper. With defeat etched deeply into her watery eyes, she would quietly ask for help to shake out the diaper into the toilet, clean her little bottom, and press the toilet handle. Then, wrapped in a neat little package, she disposed of the soiled diaper.

Wanting so badly to overcome her struggle, Isabelle became an accomplished swimmer for the next two years; she learned how to ride a bike, count to one hundred, recite the entire alphabet, and draw the birds from the northern and southern regions of the United States and actually read their names. She sounded out the names of the golden-crowned kinglet of the north and the sharp-shinned hawk of the southern part of the country (she never let the hyphen in both names throw her off). Isabelle's curiosity of the great big world was a treasure to her family, yet ...

Isabelle just couldn't bring herself to go number two unless it was in a diaper that she could shake out in the big toilet and drop into a garbage can.

Although praised, hugged, and encouraged, she just couldn't let go of her fear! Isabelle's mom, given good-intentioned advice from Isabelle's pediatrician, stopped at the nearest shopping mall on their way home from the doctor's office and purchased a little pink potty. Isabelle and her mom were excited to go home and have Isabelle give it a try!

One weekend, her grandparents arranged to have Isabelle for "two sleeps." They were very excited for their time together. Her mom brought all the important things needed for a perfect two-day stay—except her little pink toddler's potty chair that Isabelle had started using as a substitute for the big toilet.

Isabelle's grandma saw the panic in her granddaughter's eyes. "Honey, it's okay. We can do this together. I'll be right here with you."

Isabelle wrapped her thin arms around her grandma's shoulders and slowly nodded.

Isabelle lifted herself onto the seat of the large white toilet bowl. Her cheeks reddened. A tear fell first from her blue eye and then from the now-puffy brown eye. A loud whimper escaped her open, quivering lips.

Her grandmother sat cross-legged on the bathroom floor rubbing Isabelle's dangling legs, cooing softly, and telling her she could do this! "Don't be afraid, Isabelle, I'm right here."

Suddenly, Isabelle began to wail! "Please, Grandma, I just want to go home!" Isabelle was petrified!
Her grandmother was helpless! Not knowing how else to help her granddaughter, she called Isabelle's mother to come get her. The sleepover had abruptly come to an end.

Much time passed before Isabelle would stay with her grandparents again. Cell phones became Isabelle's and her grandma's way of sharing giggles and exchanging "I love you's" nearly every day. The end button on Grandma's phone could never be pressed until Isabelle was reassured how very proud her entire family was of all her accomplishments at such a young age!

"Magically, when you least expect it, Isabelle, you will just sit on the big toilet and all your fears will disappear. I promise!" Barely audible, Isabelle responded, "Are you sure, Grandma?

Summer waned too quickly as Isabelle anxiously anticipated kindergarten. Lined neatly on plastic hangers in her closet, outfits of many designs and colors hung waiting for Isabelle to choose the one that would carry her bouncing off to her very first day of school. She even had a book bag of Carolina blue and brown with speckles, matching her eyes. Isabelle could barely contain her excitement!

Except she still hadn't been able to conquer her fear. She had the same thought over and over: What will I do if I need to use the toilet at school?

Two nights before school started Isabelle's mom and dad drew her blankets tightly around her small frame, folded their hands in prayer, and kissed Isabelle good night. Isabelle drifted off into a fitful sleep. Even the big, perfectly round, smiling yellow moon couldn't ease Isabelle's worries. The thought of all her new classmates being able to use a big toilet had her stomach tied in knots!

Poor little Isabelle awoke the next day. Holding tightly with one hand to the stair railing, rubbing her swollen, puffy eyes with the other, she quietly crept down the stairs and climbed glumly into her seat at the table. She stared at her blueberry waffles, always her favorite breakfast, unable to take a bite. Then, suddenly, to her surprise, Isabelle felt an incredible urge to leave the table. She jumped off her chair, told her mom she'd be right back, and sprinted to her bathroom.

Isabelle's mom began clearing the plates, thinking this was going to be another morning that Isabelle was too sad to eat her breakfast and it wasn't worth arguing with her daughter about. But! This morning, the day before school started, wasn't going to be anything like so many other mornings these last weeks before the new school year began.

First, from the bathroom came a loud screech! This was followed by what sounded like uncontrolled chuckling! Then, the most distinct noise of all—an excited, "Mom! Mom! Come here quick!"

Isabelle's mom threw the plates into the sink and ran upstairs, skipping every other step! She threw open the bathroom door to see Isabelle jumping up and down and pointing to the water in the toilet bowl.

"Mom! Look! I did it! I went number two in the big person's toilet!"

In a single night, under the watchful eye of her friend, the moon, Isabelle, now six years old, had decided it was time to let go of all the horrible visions of going number two that she had picked up as a toddler. It was time to show the world that Isabelle was a strong, capable young lady who was ready to go to kindergarten.

Isabelle picked up her mom's cell phone and pushed the contact for Isabelle's grandparents. When her grandmother answered, Isabelle squealed excitedly, "Grandma, I went number two in the big toilet! This is my best day ever!"

Isabelle proudly went number two and then dressed herself in her new purple top with matching purple-flowered skirt, complete with black jacket and her favorite black converse tennis shoes so proudly purchased by her grandparents, for this very special day!

Grabbing her backpack off the hook by the front door, Isabelle squeezed her mom hard around the waist and yelled, "Dad, come on! Hurry! I don't want to be late for my first day of Kindergarten!"

www.ingramcontent.com/pod-product-compliance
Lightning Source LLC
LaVergne TN
LVHW071651060526
838200LV00029B/430